SIR CEDRIC

Roy Gerrard

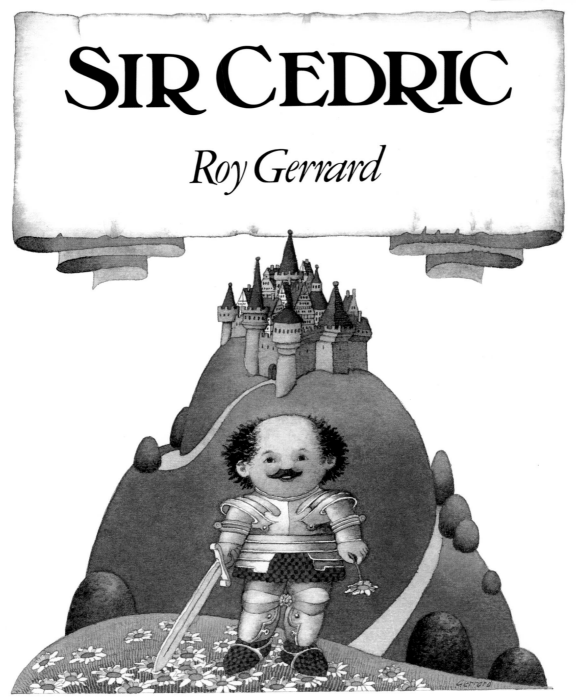

A SUNBURST BOOK · FARRAR, STRAUS AND GIROUX

Sir Cedric was cheerful and gallant,
    Sir Cedric was gentle but bold.
He ruled his lands wisely and fairly
    and was very well-liked, so I'm told.
The people who lived near his castle
    were happy to be in his care—
For robbers and villains all kept well away
    when they knew that Sir Cedric was there.
He never was rude to his subjects,
    nor mean when their taxes were due,
Nor did he go kissing their daughters
    as some wicked knights used to do.
Each morning he rode from his castle
    on Walter, his faithful old steed.
He went round the countryside sorting things out
    and checking what people might need.
But he sat in his castle one evening,
    and polished his armour and sword,
And decided that life was so peaceful and calm,
    he was getting quite restless and bored.

He thought he would go on a journey
    to find some adventure and fun,
For he'd heard there were lots of new things to be seen
    and many brave deeds to be done.
He sent for his trusty friend Bertram
    and told him just what he had planned.
Bert said he'd look after the castle
    and Cedric said, "That'll be grand."
He took up his sword and his shield and his lance
    and his armour all shiny and new,
And in case he got hungry while riding along,
    he took cucumber sandwiches too.

The people he met on the long country road
passed him by with a smile and a wave
And said they'd not seen such a very fine knight,
so handsome and sturdy and brave.

Old Walter went on for mile after mile.
    He strode up the hills at a trot.
Cedric would stop to give him a rest
    in case he got breathless and hot.
They rode through a huge gloomy forest,
    a hundred miles wide, it would seem,
In the middle of which was a large open space
    with a tower, and a bridge, and a stream.
Four square on the bridge stood a fierce-looking knight
    who was known far and wide as Black Ned.
He had Fat Matilda locked up in his tower
    and he'd threatened to chop off her head.
Matilda, though fat, was a princess, you see
    and could have any man that she chose
But Black Ned was bad-tempered, dirty and mean
    and had hairs growing out of his nose.

"These lands are all mine," said evil Black Ned.
　"If you wish to pass through, we must fight."
"It seems a bit silly," Sir Cedric replied,
　"But if you insist, well, all right."
They charged at each other with furious speed
　and met with a horrible crash.
Ned was knocked from his saddle right into the stream.
　He went down with a terrible splash.
Matilda clapped loudly to see Ned brought low.
　"Bravely done, bold Sir Knight," she observed.
Ned crawled to the bank and ran dripping away,
　which was no more than what he deserved.

Then Matilda rode off with Sir Cedric,
  and thanked him for saving her life.
She said that Black Ned would have killed her,
  when she told him she'd not be his wife.
They got on so well that the miles flew by—
  and the journey did not seem too long.
She thrilled to the clasp of his muscular arm.
  (He was little, but wiry and strong.)

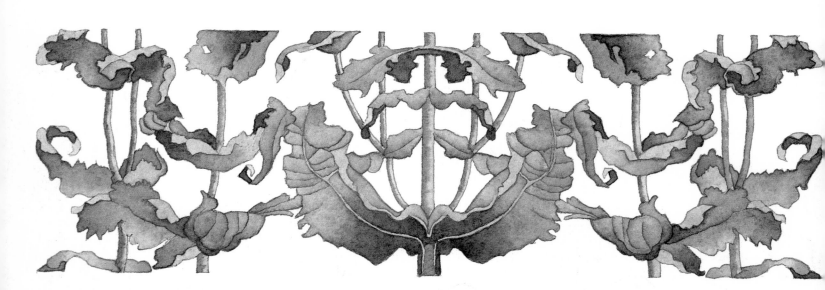

The King and Queen were overjoyed
  to see their sweet Matilda.
They thought by now Black Ned had either
  married her or killed her.
They thanked Sir Cedric gratefully
  and said that he must stay
To keep Matilda company
  and have a holiday.

Matilda grew fond of Sir Cedric.
  They rode and picnicked together.
They happily roamed through woods and lanes
  in beautiful summer weather.
They ate fresh cucumber sandwiches
  and drank home-made blackberry wine.
She thought that he was a wonderful man
  and he thought that she was divine.

Then Cedric proposed to Matilda—
    he asked if she would be his wife.
He promised her all sorts of diamonds and things
    and love that would last her for life.
I suppose you can guess that Matilda said yes
    and Sir Cedric felt likely to burst.
He said, "Let's go away and get married today."
    She said, "Let's tell my Mum and Dad first."

The King and his Queen were delighted,
   and readily gave their consent.
They held a great feast and told all their friends
   of the forthcoming happy event.

The feast was a joyous occasion,
    and the future seemed rosy and bright.
But just then a messenger burst through the door
    and his news put them all in a fright.
He said, "Black Ned has gathered an army.
    He's rapidly coming this way
To take his revenge on Sir Cedric
    and to carry Matilda away."
The guests started making excuses.
    Some said they had gardens to tend.
Some said they had cattle to care for.
    Some said they had fences to mend.
Some said they were troubled with illness.
    Some said that they had to appear
At another important engagement,
    whilst others were speechless with fear.

Then Cedric jumped up on a table.
    He shouted out, "Listen to me.
If you don't stop behaving like cowards,
    you'll never be happy and free.
For Ned is that kind of a fellow
    who likes to push people around,
And if you don't stop them, they only get worse.
    At least, that's what I've always found.
So take up your swords and your armour
    and come forth with me to the fight."
At this they all plucked up their courage,
    for they knew that Sir Cedric was right.

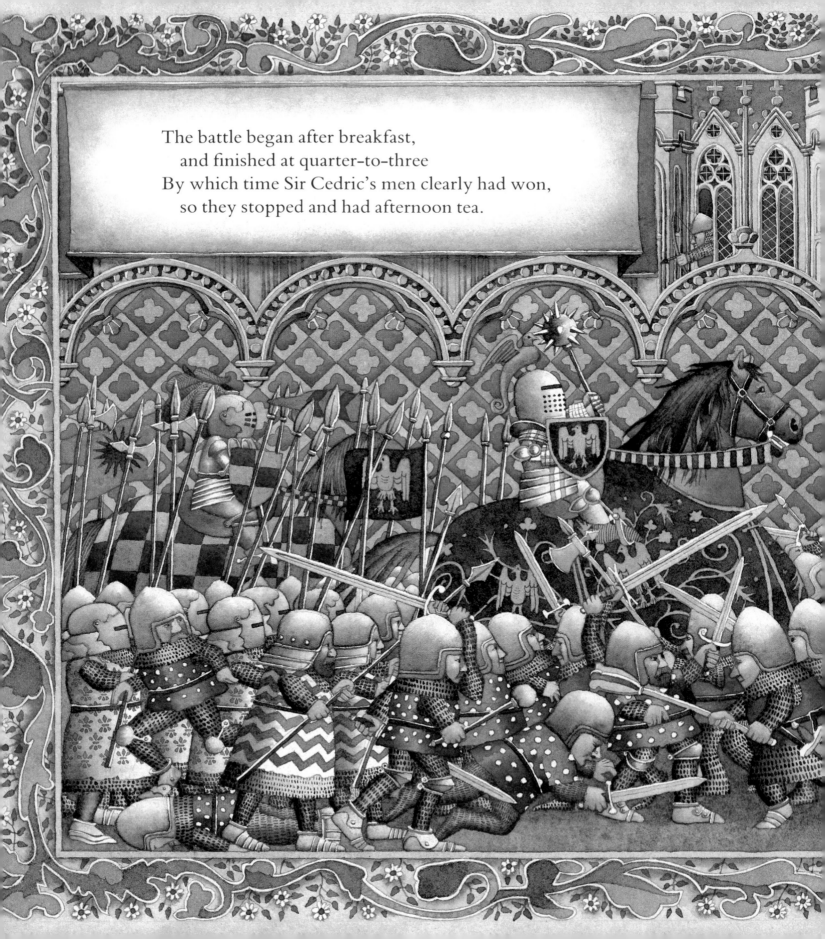

The battle began after breakfast,
   and finished at quarter-to-three
By which time Sir Cedric's men clearly had won,
   so they stopped and had afternoon tea.

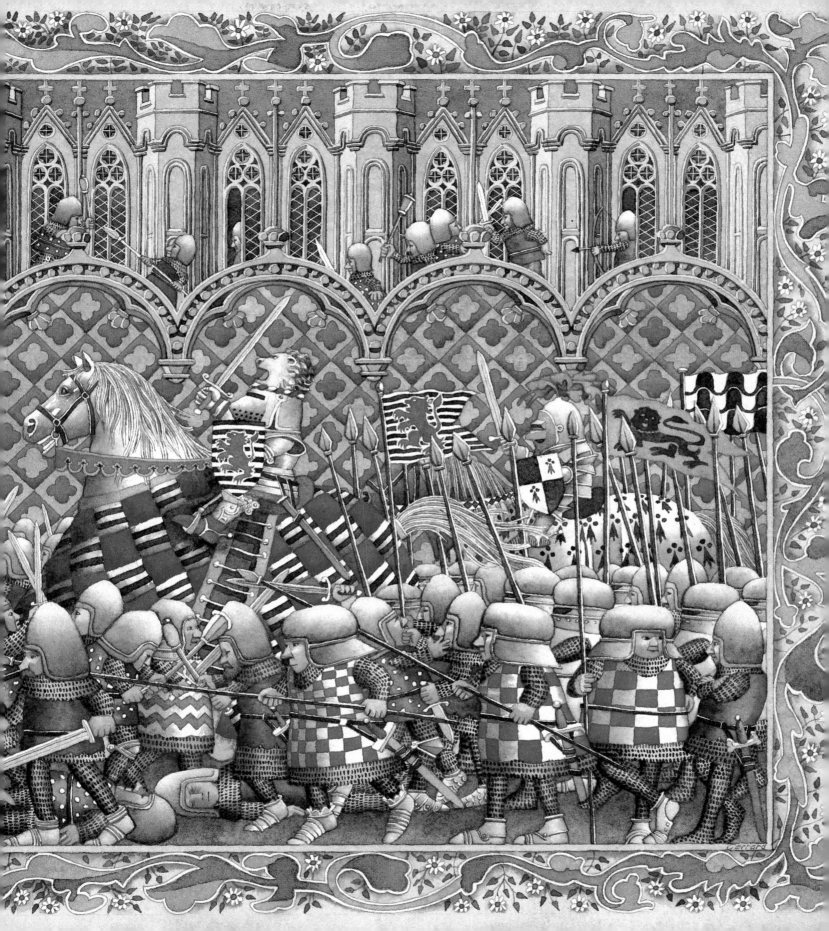

Black Ned was defeated and captured.
    The rest of his men ran away.
He was taken to Cedric, and all waited
    to hear what that brave knight would say.
He put down his cucumber sandwich
    and spoke very sharply to Ned.
"Regard yourself lucky I don't have you killed,
    for some think you'd be better off dead.
You've been bullying people for ages,
    and you've always been wicked and cruel.
Now you've lost the fight and you've lost your men
    and you've made yourself look a right fool.
Just this once you can go on your way,
    now that we've shown you who's boss
But if you should start trouble again
    I'll come back and I won't half be cross."
Black Ned was delighted and grateful
    that Cedric was setting him free
And from that day on he changed his bad ways
    and was gentle as gentle could be.

Then plans went ahead for the marriage
   and people turned up by the score
To witness the wedding of Cedric the Good
   as he married Matilda the Pure.
And after the service was over,
   they went to the castle to dine.
There was dancing and feasting with cucumber
   sandwiches, fruit cake and blackberry wine.

Goodbye to the gallant Sir Cedric.
    Goodbye to Matilda as well.
The rest of their life was so peaceful
    that there isn't much story to tell.
But if people were more like Sir Cedric—
    so modest, polite and yet brave—
Then the world would be nicer to live in
    and bullies would have to behave.
So don't go around having tantrums
    and fighting like Ned used to do.
I think people who act in this fashion
    need a very sharp lesson, don't you?